W9-AZT-498
I like Books
Chantelle Cheng 2000
WESTMINSTER SCHOOLS

Aggie's Home

AGGIE'S HOME

Joan Lowery Nixon

DELACORTE PRESS

With gratitude to two outstanding editors,
Karen Meyers and Kim Stitzel

PUBLISHED BY DELACORTE PRESS
Bantam Doubleday Dell Publishing Group, Inc.
1540 Broadway
New York, New York 10036

Library of Congress Cataloging-in-Publication Data

Nixon, Joan Lowery.
Aggie's home / Joan Lowery Nixon.
p. cm.—(Orphan train children ; [bk. #3])
Summary: A clumsy twelve-year-old, Aggie is sure no one will want to adopt her when she rides the orphan train out west, but when she meets the eccentric Bradon family she begins to have some hope. Includes historical information about orphan trains and the woman's suffrage movement.
ISBN 0-385-32295-X
[1. Orphans—Fiction. 2. Individuality—Fiction. 3. Orphan trains—Fiction. 4. Women—Suffrage—Fiction.]
I. Title. II. Series: Nixon, Joan Lowery. Orphan train children ; bk. 3.
PZ7.N65Ag 1998
[Fic]—dc21 97-47760
CIP
AC

Manufactured in the United States of America
September 1998
BVG 10 9 8 7 6 5 4 3 2 1

A Note from the Author

In the 1850s there were many homeless children in New York City. The Children's Aid Society, which was founded by Charles Loring Brace, tried to help these children by giving them new homes. They were sent west and placed with families who lived on farms and in small towns throughout the United States. From 1854 to 1929, groups of homeless children traveled on trains that were soon nicknamed orphan trains. The children were called orphan train riders.

The characters in these stories are fictional, but their problems and joys, their worries and fears, and their desire to love and be loved were experienced by the real orphan train riders of many years ago.

Joan Lowery Nixon

More orphan train stories by
Joan Lowery Nixon

The Orphan Train Adventures

A FAMILY APART
Winner of the Golden Spur Award
CAUGHT IN THE ACT
IN THE FACE OF DANGER
Winner of the Golden Spur Award
A PLACE TO BELONG
A DANGEROUS PROMISE
KEEPING SECRETS
CIRCLE OF LOVE

ORPHAN TRAIN CHILDREN

LUCY'S WISH
WILL'S CHOICE
AGGIE'S HOME

Homes Wanted

For Children

A Company of Orphan Children

of different ages in charge of an agent will arrive at your town on date herein mentioned. The object of the coming of these children is to find homes in your midst, especially among farmers, where they may enjoy a happy and wholesome family life, where kind care, good example and moral training will fit them for a life of self-support and usefulness. They come under the auspices of the New York Children's Aid Society. They have been tested and found to be well-meaning boys and girls anxious for homes.

The conditions are that these children shall be properly clothed, treated as members of the family, given proper school advantages and remain in the family until they are eighteen years of age. At the expiration of the time specified it is hoped that arrangements can be made whereby they may be able to remain in the family indefinitely. The Society retains the right to remove a child at any time for just cause, and agrees to remove any found unsatisfactory after being notified.

Remember the time and place. All are invited. Come out and hear the address. Applications may be made to any one of the following well known citizens, who have agreed to act as local committee to aid the agent in securing homes.

A. J. Hammond, H. W. Parker, Geo. Baxter, J. F. Damon, J. P. Humes,
H. N. Welch, J. A. Armstrong, F. L. Durgin.

This distribution of Children is by Consent of the State Board of Control, and will take place at the

G. A. R. Hall, Winnebago, Minn.

Friday, Jan. 11th, '07, at 10.30 a. m. & 2 p. m.

H. D. Clarke, State Agent,
Dodge Center, Minn.

Office: 105 East 22nd St.,
New York City.

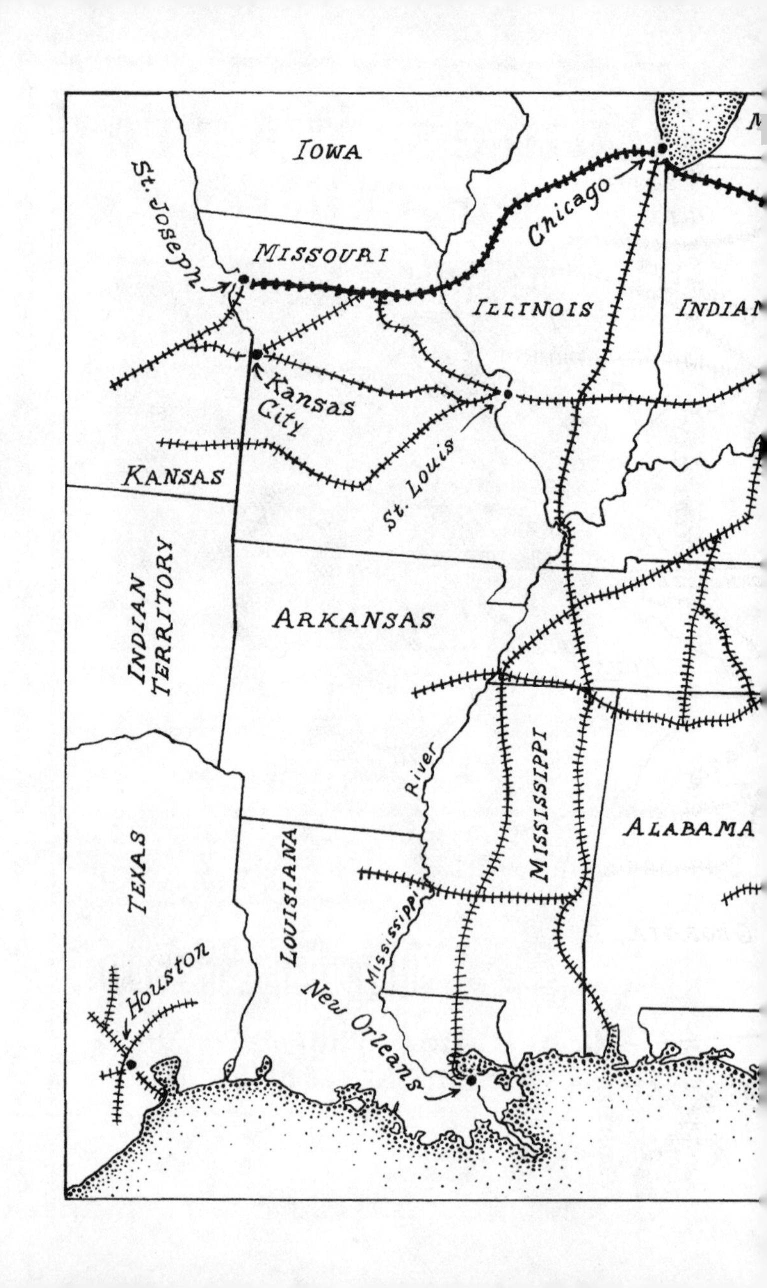
IOWA
St. Joseph
MISSOURI
Chicago
ILLINOIS
INDIAN
Kansas City
St. Louis
KANSAS
INDIAN TERRITORY
ARKANSAS
River
MISSISSIPPI
ALABAMA
TEXAS
LOUISIANA
Mississippi
Houston
New Orleans

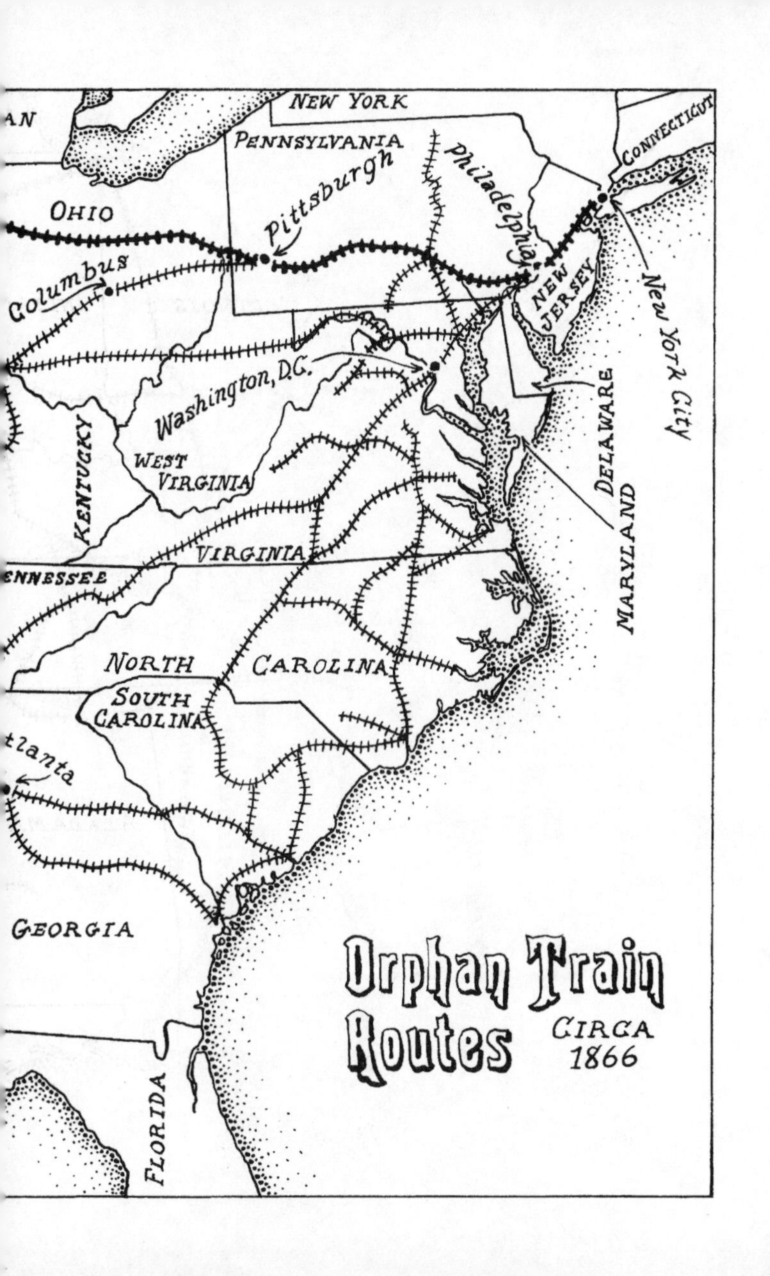

NEW YORK
AN
PENNSYLVANIA
Pittsburgh
Philadelphia
CONNECTICUT
OHIO
Columbus
NEW JERSEY
New York City
Washington, D.C.
DELAWARE
KENTUCKY
WEST VIRGINIA
MARYLAND
VIRGINIA
ENNESSEE
NORTH
CAROLINA
SOUTH CAROLINA
tlanta
GEORGIA
FLORIDA
Orphan Train Routes
CIRCA 1866

From the Journal of
FRANCES MARY KELLY, JULY 1866

I do not worry about finding homes for most of the children I am escorting on this orphan train. They are lively, handsome children, and I know they will find foster parents. But when I look at Aggie Vaughn, my heart aches.

At twelve, Aggie is tall for her age. She has moments in which she can be quite clumsy and ungainly—all elbows and knees. Her hair had been chopped short while she lived in the Asylum for Homeless Waifs. Although her hair has grown some and has been trimmed, there is no way to make it look attractive. I can only pray that a loving couple will look within Aggie to discover her many fine qualities.

With all her heart Aggie wants a family to take her in. She's afraid if she is not chosen, she'll be returned to the orphan asylum and its director, Mrs. Marchlander. But I hope that Aggie will drop the wall she has built to protect herself.

"I never cry," Aggie told me bravely. "Even when I broke a rule and had to go without supper. Even when

Mrs. Marchlander beat my hands with a ruler and told me no one would ever want to adopt me, I was never afraid, and I never cried."

"I'm sorry that someone hurt you," I said. I tried to take one of her hands, but Aggie pulled away.

"No need to feel sorry for me," Aggie said. "I learned my lesson. I'll never, never let anyone hurt me again. That's what I told Mrs. Marchlander, and that's why she sent me away."

Aggie's backbone stiffened. "Mrs. Marchlander said I was a waif—somebody no one wants. But someone will want me because . . ."

I prompted, "Because?"

Aggie didn't answer my question, but the expression on her face told me that she had a secret she wasn't going to share. All I can guess is that this secret has given Aggie the inner strength she needs.

CHAPTER ONE

Agatha Mae Vaughn twisted around on the seat of the wagon for one last look at the Asylum for Homeless Waifs. How she hated the name of that place! She was glad to be leaving.

Aggie thought about a day soon after she'd arrived at the asylum. It had been a finding-out day. A day in which she'd discovered a secret all her own.

She'd been eight years old then. She'd been sent from the foundling home in New Jersey, where very young children without parents were cared for, to the asylum to live.

She had spent much of her first week at the asylum in Mrs. Marchlander's office. No matter how hard Aggie tried to follow the long list of rules that had been read to her, she found herself breaking them. On the day that turned out to be the special day, Aggie had been sent to Mrs. Marchlander for running in the hallway.

"I ran because lessons had started and I was late," Aggie explained.

"That is no excuse," Mrs. Marchlander said.

"But I had to help Sonya tie her shoes. She's only four."

Mrs. Marchlander glared down her nose at Aggie. "And you're eight—old enough to know the rules. Now, sit down on that bench and wait—I have an important visitor."

Squirming on the hard bench outside Mrs. Marchlander's office, Aggie couldn't help hearing the conversation going on inside.

We must be getting a new matron, Aggie thought. Mrs. Marchlander was busy explaining so many things to the woman.

"There's a file for each of the children in that cabinet near the door," Mrs. Marchlander said. "There you'll find records of their health, of their progress in their schoolwork, and any information about their families."

Aggie slumped on the bench. Families? She didn't have a family. When she had asked at the foundling home, she'd been told that she had been abandoned on the steps when she was only a few days old.

And when Aggie asked, "Can I leave the asylum when somebody comes to adopt me?" Mrs. Marchlander shook her head.

"No one is likely to want you, Aggie," she said. "Most people who come ask for babies. Others want obedient, older girls who are hard workers—not troublemakers, as you seem to be."

Frowning, Aggie pushed the awful memory aside and listened to what Mrs. Marchlander was telling the new matron.

"The files include anything known about the children," Mrs. Marchlander explained. "Perhaps a baptismal certificate, a note about the date of the child's birth, information about the parents. You do understand that these records must be kept secret, especially from the children."

Are there any notes about me? Aggie wondered. Her curiosity quickly turned to determination. *If there are, I'm going to find them.*

The new matron left the office, walking past Aggie without even a curious glance.

Mrs. Marchlander called Aggie back into her office and sternly shook her head. "You waifs must learn to follow rules."

"I'm *not* a waif," Aggie insisted. "I'm me—Aggie."

"And you were caught running in the hallway," Mrs. Marchlander said. "Hold out your hands, Aggie. It's time for your punishment."

Aggie winced as the wooden ruler stung her palms again and again. Each time she'd been punished, she'd tried not to cry. But the ruler hurt so much, she couldn't help it. It wasn't until she burst into tears that Mrs. Marchlander placed the ruler back on her desk.

"Sit here for one half hour and compose yourself," Mrs. Marchlander ordered. Her tight smile returned. "That means you will miss the noon meal. However, it is far better for you to think about your behavior than about food."

Mrs. Marchlander tidied her desk, dropped her ring of keys into the top drawer, and left for her own lunch.

Aggie sat quietly, head down, until she heard the heels of Mrs. Marchlander's shoes clicking away down the stairway. She knew this was her only chance. She raced to Mrs. Marchlander's desk, opened the top drawer, and grabbed the keys. As quickly as she could, she tested them with trembling fingers until she found the one that unlocked the file cabinet.

The names of the children had been filed alphabetically. It took only a moment for Aggie to find the large brown envelope with her name on it. Eagerly she opened it and spread the papers on a nearby table.

Near the bottom of the pile of papers was a form from the foundling home in New Jersey. It listed Aggie's full name and her date of birth.

"May first!" Aggie said aloud, and then she

clapped a hand over her mouth. Mrs. Marchlander had told Aggie that no one knew her birth date. She had lied. Aggie did have a birthday! A real birthday!

Clipped to the back of the form was a small sheet of paper. On it, in rounded, delicate handwriting, was written:

This is my daughter, Agatha Mae Vaughn, born ten days ago on the first of May, in the year 1854. Please give her your loving care. It breaks my heart to give her up to strangers, but I am in temporary distress. As soon as I am able, I shall return to claim Agatha, because I love her dearly and always will.

The note was unsigned.

Aggie could feel the pounding of her heart, and she could hear voices in the distance. But she stood in a world apart, the warmth of her mother's love wrapped snugly around her. *I had a mother, and she loved me,* Aggie thought. *And she always will.*

Mrs. Marchlander's voice snapped Aggie from her dream.

Chapter Two

Terrified, Aggie stuffed the note into the pocket of her white cotton apron. She returned the papers to the brown envelope and quickly shoved it back into the file. Locking the file cabinet and dropping the keys into Mrs. Marchlander's desk, Aggie flopped back in her seat only seconds before Mrs. Marchlander and the new matron entered the office.

"You may leave, Aggie. Go directly to the sewing room," Mrs. Marchlander said. She didn't even look at Aggie.

Breathlessly Aggie left the office and walked—careful not to run—to the room where the girls spent their afternoon hours sewing and mending.

Aggie hated sewing and usually let her mind

wander to other things. That day she thought about her mother. Aggie had been right. She wasn't a waif. She had a mother who loved her, and she had a real birth date. She was Agatha Mae Vaughn. Her mother had given her that name, and no one—not even Mrs. Marchlander—could take that away from her.

From that day on Aggie was sure that someday her mother would come for her. The note was a promise, and Aggie knew her mother would keep her promise if she could. Aggie hid the note, taking it out to read during the times when she needed to know that someone loved her.

What would her mother look like? She wouldn't be anything like Mrs. Marchlander with her thin lips and her gray-streaked hair pulled back into a tight bun. Aggie's mother would be young and kind and gentle. Her eyes would sparkle when she laughed. And when Aggie was sad or lonely, her mother would wrap her arms around her and hug her close.

It's all right, Aggie would tell herself. *Someday my*

mother will come for me. Someday I'll see her beautiful face.

Aggie didn't mean to be difficult. But over the next four years it sometimes seemed as though everything she did landed her in trouble with Mrs. Marchlander.

"Aggie, you were caught peeking through the bars of the front gate. You know that is not allowed."

"I was watching Ezra sell a horse," Aggie had said. "Do you know that people who want to buy a horse check its teeth first? Ezra says if the teeth are worn down, the horse might be old or in bad health."

Mrs. Marchlander had shaken her head impatiently. "Tonight you'll have no supper," she'd replied.

Not long after Aggie's twelfth birthday, Mrs. Marchlander had told her, "Aggie, you know that talking is not allowed, except at your half-hour recreation period each day. This is the third time this week you have been scolded for speaking during the sewing period."

Aggie had shrugged. "Sewing is boring. Talking makes it fun."

Mrs. Marchlander waved away Aggie's words. "You are to learn the trade of a seamstress. The work you do brings income to the asylum. You cannot work at taking neat and tiny stitches if you're engaged in idle chatter. I'm afraid that you'll go without your supper again. And once more I'll have to use the ruler."

Mrs. Marchlander's lips became a tight line as she picked up her ruler. "You are sent to me for discipline far too often, Aggie. One more time, and I'll have to take stronger measures. Hold out your hands."

Tears flooded Aggie's eyes as the ruler stung her palms. *Oh, Mother, where are you?* she wondered. *Please, please, come for me soon.*

One day Aggie made up a funny song about the way the girls had to wash their faces and their cropped hair every morning with lye soap and cold water.

"We rub off our hair and rub off our skins, while Mrs. Marchlander laughs and grins," Aggie sang. The girls giggled, but the matron in charge was shocked. She rushed Aggie to Mrs. Marchlander's office.

"Hold out your hands," Mrs. Marchlander ordered. She began to beat Aggie's palms with her ruler.

Aggie clenched her teeth against the pain. *Mother, help me,* she said over and over in her mind. This time the tears didn't come.

"What's the matter with you, Aggie? Why don't you cry?" Mrs. Marchlander shouted in fury. As she slashed the ruler down across Aggie's palms once again, it snapped in two.

Aggie slowly brought down her hands and held them at her sides. Although the pain was terrible, she glared at Mrs. Marchlander. "This is the last time you'll hit me," she said. "I won't let you hit me again. And I'll never again let you see me cry."

Now Aggie was leaving the asylum. By challenging Mrs. Marchlander, Aggie knew that she had brought more trouble on her head than she had planned.

Aggie made a face in the direction of Mrs. Marchlander's office window. She hoped Mrs. Marchlander was looking out the window and would see it. She hated the asylum, and she hated Mrs. Marchlander, too.

Aggie turned to Ezra, who held the horses's reins, and asked, "Where are we going?"

Ezra's answer was only a grunt.

Aggie slumped back on the seat. *Where are you, Mother?* she thought. *You said you would come for me.*

Chapter Three

The wagon stopped in front of a dark brick building. Aggie sighed as she read the sign over the door: THE CHILDREN'S AID SOCIETY. Was this just one more orphan asylum with its bread and gruel and mean matron?

A plump woman with a broad smile opened the door in response to Ezra's knock.

"This here is Aggie Vaughn," Ezra said. He held out an envelope. "And these are her records."

"Thank you," the woman answered. She beamed at Aggie and said, "I'm Miss Hunter, Aggie. We've been expecting you. Please come in."

Aggie edged through the open door, but stiffened as Miss Hunter reached out to take her hand. "Before you tell me your rules, I'm going to tell you mine," Aggie said. "My rule is, nobody's ever going to hit me again."

Miss Hunter's eyes widened in surprise. "Dear child," she said, "no one here will ever hurt you."

"Even if I live here for a long time?" Aggie asked. "Even if I break one of your rules?"

"Didn't anyone tell you about the Children's Aid Society and what we do?" Miss Hunter asked.

Aggie shook her head.

Miss Hunter smiled again. "You won't be staying with us for long, Aggie. We're going to find you a home."

"You mean a home in which I'll work? Scrub floors? Cook? Sew?"

"No, I mean a home with two parents who will choose you to care for. You'll have a family."

"A family?" Aggie repeated. It was hard to believe. She'd been told no one would want her, so she hadn't dared to dream. She had no idea what it would be like to have a home and parents. And she still hoped that someday her mother would find her.

Miss Hunter put an arm around Aggie's shoulders. Aggie flinched, uncomfortable at her touch. Miss Hunter gently guided Aggie into a small parlor. There she told her about the orphan trains that took children to towns in the West to find foster parents.

When Miss Hunter had finished, she took a good look at Aggie's dark, heavy cotton dress with its coverall apron. "We'll give you new clothing," she told Aggie. "But we'll start by assigning you to a bed in one of our dormitory rooms, and we'll give you some supper. There aren't many children here now, because a group left just last week for their journey west. But soon there will be more company for you."

As she reached out and gently touched Aggie's short hair, she said, "Your hair will grow out a little by the time the next group leaves. Maybe with a bow, or a little lace cap . . ."

Aggie caught a glimpse of herself in the mirror that hung over a table by the door. There had been no mirrors at the asylum, so she hadn't given a thought to what she looked like. She bit her lip, wishing she still didn't know. Pale skin, choppy, uneven hair—*Maybe Mrs. Marchlander was right,* Aggie realized. *Who could possibly want someone who looks like me?*

For the next two months Aggie lived at the Children's Aid Society. By then twenty-nine other children had arrived. One of them was Mary Beth Lansdown, a pretty girl with long, shining hair.

Miss Hunter introduced Mary Beth to Aggie and said, "Now you'll have a friend close to your age."

As Miss Hunter walked away, Mary Beth stared at Aggie's head. "What happened to your hair?" she asked.

Aggie's face grew hot with embarrassment. "My hair's growing," she said.

"But it's so short." Mary Beth gasped. "Did it fall out? Did you have a terrible disease?"

Aggie put her hands on Mary Beth's head and made a horrible face. "Yes," she said. "It was awful. And it's catching!"

Mary Beth shrieked and ran from the room.

In a few minutes Miss Hunter came to Aggie. "You were rude to Mary Beth," she said. "Perhaps you should apologize."

"No," Aggie said. "She was the rude one."

Miss Hunter sighed. "I was hoping that you and Mary Beth might become friends," she said. "It would be good for you to have a friend."

Aggie shook her head. "I don't need a friend," she answered.

That night Aggie heard Mary Beth snuffling under her blanket. She felt bad, wondering if Mary Beth was crying because she'd been mean. Aggie wanted to comfort Mary Beth, to tell her that she had nothing to worry about. Mary Beth was pretty. She wouldn't have any trouble finding a family who would want her.

But Aggie rolled over and pulled her own blanket over her ears. She couldn't comfort Mary Beth, because she was scared about the upcoming trip too. Who knew what would really happen when they were sent west?

After supper the next day Miss Hunter called all the children together. She introduced them to a young woman named Frances Mary Kelly. Miss Kelly smiled at them as though they were already friends.

Everyone laughed when two-year-old Lizzie Ann Schultz held up her arms to Miss Kelly and said, "Mama."

Miss Hunter said, "Mary Beth, how would you like to be paired with Lizzie on the trip? You can help care for her."

Mary Beth smiled proudly. "Lizzie likes to have me hold her," she said.

Without thinking, Aggie angrily blurted out, "Miss Hunter, you should have asked *me* to take care of her. I'm the oldest."

"Oh, dear. I know you are, Aggie," Miss Hunter said. "But I thought—"

Miss Kelly stepped up and put an arm around Aggie's shoulders. Aggie stiffened, but Miss Kelly didn't seem to notice.

"Aggie," she said, "I hereby make you my official

assistant. I'll need you to help me with *all* the little ones."

"Aggie can't tell us what to do," one of the younger boys said.

"Of course not," Miss Kelly told him. "She won't even try. She'll be helping me feed everyone during the day, make them comfortable at night, count noses at depot stops. . . . There's a great deal Aggie and I will have to do together."

Aggie felt her cheeks grow warm. Miss Kelly was trusting her. She had given her an important job. *I can do it,* Aggie thought. *I'll show her that I can do it well.* Maybe, if she was especially good, a real family would want to adopt her.

Miss Kelly smiled and said, "I was an orphan train rider too. When I was Aggie's age, I traveled to St. Joseph, Missouri, with my brothers, Mike, Danny, and Pete, and my sisters, Megan and Peg."

Aggie listened to Miss Kelly with newfound hope. She couldn't believe that a lady like Miss Kelly had once been a scared young girl in search of a family. For the first time in a long time, Aggie smiled.

Maybe she really *would* find a family that wanted her, just as Miss Kelly had. Then she could forget about Mrs. Marchlander and orphan asylums and everything else . . . except the mother who had always loved her.

Chapter Four

At first riding on the train was exciting. There were new things to discover. Aggie had never seen fruit growing on trees or cows in a field.

But soot from the engine's smokestack soon blew through the train's open windows, and the wooden seats grew hard and uncomfortable. By late morning some of the little children had begun to cry, including Lizzie. She squirmed on Mary Beth's lap and whimpered.

Aggie held out her hands. "I'll take Lizzie for a while," she said to Mary Beth.

"No, you won't. I'm taking care of her, not you." Mary Beth tightened her arms around Lizzie.

"She's crying because she's hungry."

"Is not. She's just fussy."

"She is too. I know what hunger crying is."

"Do not."

Aggie walked down the aisle to where Miss Kelly was seated. "Some of the little children are getting hungry," she said. "Like Lizzie. Mary Beth said I didn't know what I was talking about, but I know when a baby gets fussy because she's hungry. I know a lot more than Mary Beth knows. And you did say I was sort of in charge. When are we going to feed the little ones?"

Miss Kelly pulled out her pocket watch and glanced at it. "It's not yet noon, but I think we're *all* getting hungry," she said. "I'll open the hamper, and if you'd like, since you're my special assistant, you can give everyone an apple—except the little ones, of course. I'll peel and chop their apples."

Aggie's mouth watered. "We get apples?" she asked. Apples were a rare treat.

"Along with bread and cheese," Miss Kelly said.

Aggie happily set to work, helping Miss Kelly give out the food. Then, after everyone had been served, Aggie bit into her apple. The sweet juice trickled onto her tongue, and she chewed slowly, wanting the apple to last as long as possible.

During the rest of the trip, Aggie tried hard to be helpful. Miss Kelly would buy fresh milk at each station, and Aggie would fill the tin cup, giving each child a drink in turn. She wiped up spills—a few she accidentally caused herself—and cleaned small faces and hands.

Aggie wanted to stay busy. When she was busy, she didn't think so much. If she wasn't busy, fears crept in, and she shivered, hugging her arms. There were thirty children in their group. Twenty-nine of them were ready to be adopted.

And then there's me, Aggie thought. *What if nobody wants me?*

As the train finally neared the orphan train riders' first stop, in Harwood, Missouri, Miss Kelly brushed everyone's hair and tied big butterfly bows in the girls' hair.

Aggie shook her head as Miss Kelly held out a ribbon. "I don't need one," she mumbled.

When they reached the station, the children left the train carrying their nightwear and a change of clothing wrapped in paper and tied with string. They marched by twos down the main street of Harwood to the Methodist church. Inside the church they were seated on a stage, facing a large audience.

Aggie tried not to pay attention to the people who stared at her. One woman pointed at Aggie's short hair and whispered something to the man next to her. They both laughed.

Miss Kelly introduced each of the children and invited people to come to the stage to meet them. Aggie watched Lizzie and some of the other younger children get chosen right away. A few of the older boys were quickly chosen too. When Mary Beth walked off the stage with smiling, new parents, Aggie ached with jealousy. The woman was young and pretty, just as Aggie imagined her own mother must be.

Suddenly a middle-aged couple stopped next to Aggie.

Eagerly she looked up at the beaky-nosed woman and her lanky husband. But Aggie flinched as she realized they were examining her as if she were a bolt of cloth.

"She's a strapping big girl," the woman said to her husband. "She's not much to look at, and that hair's a sight, but I'm sure she can handle plenty of hard work."

The woman suddenly took Aggie's upper arm in her rough hands and squeezed it.

Aggie jerked her arm away in fear and anger. "Don't touch me!" she snapped at the woman.

"Well, I never!" the woman exclaimed. "Hard worker or not, I don't want a rude child like you!"

Aggie willed herself not to cry as the woman and her husband stomped off the stage.

Miss Kelly stepped up and put an arm around Aggie's shoulders. "Pay no attention to people like that," she said.

"I don't want to go with them," Aggie insisted.

"You don't have to," Miss Kelly told her.

Aggie's eyes burned, and her throat ached. "I—I

don't want to be kitchen help. I want somebody to love me."

"Somebody will," Miss Kelly said.

"Maybe Mrs. Marchlander was right. Maybe no one can love me."

"Aggie, dear, forget Mrs. Marchlander. She was wrong," Miss Kelly said. "Forget these people who were rude to you. I wouldn't have let you go with them in any case. You weren't sent here to be an unpaid worker. You were sent to be part of a loving family. Look for the family who will choose you. If you see people coming to talk to you, smile at them. I know you must have a beautiful smile."

"Smile just so they'll choose me? That's like begging. I can't do that! I can't!"

"Then smile because *you'd* choose *them.* Can you try?"

Aggie lifted her face to look into Miss Kelly's eyes. "I guess I can try," she said.

And she did try, but no one else came near, and soon the last of the visitors had left.

Aggie counted the children who hadn't been chosen. Some of them sat alone. A few of them clung to each other. "There are twelve of us no one wanted," Aggie said to Miss Kelly.

Behind Aggie, someone sobbed.

Miss Kelly said, "Don't worry, children. There are two more stops scheduled. The right families will be waiting for you."

Chapter Five

It was a short ride to Springbrook, the second stop. Every time Aggie thought about being looked over by strangers again, her breathing quickened and her heart began to pound.

As the train neared the station, Miss Kelly retied drooping hair ribbons. Again she held out a ribbon to Aggie. "I've got a lovely white ribbon that would match the collar on your dress," she said.

Aggie shook her head angrily. "I don't need a ribbon. Are people going to want me just because I'm wearing a ribbon? People aren't supposed to want to adopt me because of what I'm like on the outside. They're supposed to care about what's on the *inside.* They're supposed to care about *me*!"

Miss Kelly bent to look directly into Aggie's eyes. "You're right," she said, "and that's the way *you're* supposed to care about *them.*"

Surprised, Aggie took a step backward. How could she care about people she didn't even know? And why should they care about her?

As Aggie thought about it, the train pulled to a stop. The children clutched their packages as Miss Kelly led them down from the car and onto the platform.

A thin-lipped woman told Miss Kelly that she was head of the placing-out committee in Springbrook. "The train will be in Springbrook for half an hour," she said, "so we'll do the choosing right here and now on the platform and get the waifs no one wants back on board."

Aggie winced. She hated that word *waifs.* It reminded her of Mrs. Marchlander.

Miss Kelly gathered the children around her. She introduced them and gave a short speech about what the Children's Aid Society expected of the foster parents.

During the talk Aggie tried to smile for Miss Kelly's sake.

But a heavyset woman leaned into Aggie's face and ordered, "Open your mouth, child. Let's have a look at your teeth."

"No! I am not a horse!" Aggie snapped.

The woman's husband scowled at Aggie and took a menacing step toward her. "There'll be no talk like that," he growled.

Aggie flinched. "Don't you dare hit me," she warned, "or I'll yell and scream and hit you back."

Miss Kelly hurried to Aggie's side and put an arm around her shoulders. "There seems to be a problem here," Miss Kelly said.

The woman drew her shawl tightly around her shoulders. "It's no wonder this child has no mother. The way she looks and acts, any self-respecting mother would be ashamed of her."

Aggie gasped. Her chest hurt, and it was hard to breathe.

"We don't want the likes of that young savage,"

the woman's husband said as the couple stomped off.

Aggie looked up at Miss Kelly. "I'm not a young savage. I'm a person. I'm Aggie. And my mother loved me." Her fingers trembled as they touched the note in her skirt pocket.

For years the note from Aggie's mother had been her special secret. She had hidden it away from everyone. But Miss Kelly was different. She was kind. She'd listen, and she'd understand.

"My mother left me on the steps of a foundling home when I was born," Aggie said. "She had to! She didn't want to leave me!"

"Of course she didn't," Miss Kelly said gently. She took Aggie's hands in hers.

"She wrote a note. She pinned it to my basket," Aggie told her. "I have it. I found it in my file in Mrs. Marchlander's office, and I took it, because it belongs to me, not her. My mother wrote that she was in temporary distress—those are the exact words. And she wrote that she would come back for me someday."

"Oh, Aggie, love." Tears filled Miss Kelly's eyes.

"It's been twelve years," Aggie said, "so I don't think she will come back. But she loved me, so maybe . . . My mother loved me, and somebody else will. Won't they?"

"Of course they will," Miss Kelly said. "Let me talk to a few of the people here."

Aggie watched Miss Kelly move from one couple to another. But each of them glanced at Aggie, shook their heads, and walked away. Aggie felt sick. She wished she could hide. Was she really as terrible as the woman had said she was?

Most of the children had been chosen by the time the engineer blew a blast on the engine's whistle. Only four children boarded the train again.

Harry Stowe, Jessie Lester, and Eddie Marsh had red eyes and faces streaked with tears. But Aggie sat stubbornly, not crying, her arms folded tightly across her chest. She didn't want to think about what would happen to her if she wasn't chosen, but she couldn't help it.

"I am *not* going back to Mrs. Marchlander," she vowed.

"Of course you're not," Miss Kelly said. "I'm

sure that there's someone in Woodridge who'll choose you and love you."

"You can't really know for sure," Jessie said. "You're just guessing."

"If we don't get chosen, will they send us back?" Eddie asked.

Aggie turned to Miss Kelly. "I'm not going back," she said again. "I'll run away first."

Chapter Six

Aggie kept to herself on the trip to Woodridge. She felt even worse than when she'd been hit by a ruler or been sent to bed without supper. She fingered the note from her mother, but even that didn't help.

Maybe I should change, she thought. *I'll be quiet and obedient. Then someone will want me.*

When the train neared Woodridge, Aggie gripped Miss Kelly's arm. "Please," she begged in a hoarse whisper, "may I have a hair ribbon?"

"Of course," Miss Kelly said, and hugged her. She pulled a white ribbon from her carpetbag and tied it around Aggie's hair. "You look lovely," she said. "And remember—you're also lovely on the inside, Aggie."

Miss Kelly smiled at all the children. "We'll find you homes, but you'll all have to help. Smile and be friendly."

"What if someone chooses us and we go with them but we don't get along?" Eddie asked.

"Then we'll take you from them and find you new homes," Miss Kelly said.

"How will you know how they're treating us?" Aggie asked.

"Andrew MacNair, an agent from the Children's Aid Society, will make a visit in a few months. He'll talk to your foster parents, and he'll talk to you. If you're unhappy, you can tell him, and he'll take you away immediately and find other foster parents for you."

Suddenly a disturbing thought came to Aggie. "What if the people who take us decide they don't want us?" she asked fearfully.

"They'll send for Mr. MacNair, and he'll find you a new home."

Aggie shivered. If a family chose her in Woodridge, she'd have to be well behaved and obedient. She'd have to be just like Mary Beth Lansdown, or she'd be sent back—maybe to Mrs. Marchlander.

On the platform Miss Kelly was met by the head of the local committee. Together they led the orphan train riders down two streets to Woodridge's school auditorium. Aggie heard a snicker and turned to see two older girls pointing at her hair. Others joined in.

At once Aggie's spirit was broken. She couldn't smile. She couldn't look anyone in the eye. She felt as if she were back in the asylum, miserable and alone.

Harry and Jessie were quickly chosen. Only Aggie and Eddie were left.

With a sick knot in her stomach, Aggie watched people drifting out of the room. This was the last stop, and no one had wanted her. What would become of her? What was she going to do?

An elderly couple entered the auditorium just as the last visitors were leaving. They paused, glanced around, and made their way directly to Aggie.

The woman walked slowly and carefully, as though she were in pain. The man held a hand under her elbow to steady her.

They smiled at Aggie, and the man said, "We're Bertha and Eldon Bradon."

"We're so glad you're here," Mrs. Bradon said to Aggie. "We wanted a girl."

Aggie felt her mouth open in surprise. "Me?" she asked. "You want *me*?"

"What's your name, child?" Mr. Bradon asked.

"Aggie. That is, it's Agatha Mae Vaughn," Aggie answered.

"A beautiful name," Mr. Bradon said.

"We live less than a mile from this school, Aggie," Mrs. Bradon told her, "and we've always felt that learning is important. So come late September, after the harvest, when school starts up again, you'll be enrolled. How do you feel about going to school?"

"I like to read, and I'm good with my numbers," Aggie answered. She'd never been to a real school, only to classes in the asylum. The idea of school was exciting.

Mr. Bradon's eyes twinkled. "I knew you would be," he said. "I could tell right off you were smart."

Mrs. Bradon rested her hand on her husband's arm. As Aggie stared at Mrs. Bradon's twisted fingers, she suspected why the Bradons had picked her. "I know why you want me. It's to do your household chores," she blurted out.

Mrs. Bradon looked surprised. "Only your share, dear," she said.

Aggie flushed in embarrassment. How could she make up for her bluntness? She had to make them see that she was a sweet, obedient girl. "I do want to help around the house," she insisted.

The Bradons smiled. "Will you come with us and be our little girl?" Mrs. Bradon asked.

Aggie took a deep breath. She glanced around the nearly empty room and then at Eddie, who huddled alone on one side of the stage. Her heart ached for Eddie. What would happen to him? What would happen to *her* if she didn't go with the Bradons?

"Yes. Thank you. I'll come with you," Aggie said, her voice shaking.

After the arrangements had been made, Aggie

threw herself at Miss Kelly, wrapping her in a good-bye hug.

"I'm sure you'll be happy with the Bradons," Miss Kelly told her.

Aggie stood up straight and held her head high. "At least I was chosen by people who wanted me. Mrs. Marchlander was wrong."

Mr. Bradon helped Aggie climb up to the front seat of the wagon. She sat between him and his wife and looked out at the patches of farmland and woods that covered the nearby hills beyond Woodridge.

"It will be so nice to have a child in the house again," Mrs. Bradon said.

Aggie didn't know how to answer. "Do you have other children?" she asked.

"Oh my yes, and two of them are still living at home," Mrs. Bradon answered. "There's Penelope, who's twenty-two, and Leon, who just turned seventeen."

"They must be a big help to you on your farm," Aggie said, surprised.

"Not so you'd notice," Mr. Bradon said. A smile flickered across his face.

"Now, Eldon, they're wonderful children," Mrs. Bradon insisted. "They're intelligent and imaginative and—"

"And at times a little frightening to the neighbors," Mr. Bradon said. He laughed.

Mrs. Bradon patted Aggie's arm. "Pay him no mind," she said. But she laughed too.

Puzzled, Aggie looked from Mrs. Bradon to Mr. Bradon and back again. What was frightening about Penelope and Leon? What kind of strange family could this be?

Chapter Seven

Mr. Bradon pulled the horse to a stop directly in front of a large white house with a wide, comfortable porch across the front. This beautiful house was to be her new home? Aggie could hardly believe it.

She had expected the mysterious Penelope and Leon to hurry out and greet their parents. Instead, a middle-aged man in work clothes stepped off the porch and strode toward them.

"Morning, Mrs. Bradon . . . Elton," he said.

"Morning, Silas," Mr. Bradon answered. "Meet our new daughter, Aggie." He turned to include Aggie in his smile and said, "Silas Hanson's farm is up the road a piece."

Mr. Hanson stopped and looked at Aggie with curiosity. "I heard you were getting one of them orphan train children. To help Bertha with her chores, no doubt."

"Nope. Just to be a daughter," Mr. Bradon said.

"Seems to me your hands are full enough with your daughter still at home," Mr. Hanson said with a frown. "You got to stop Penelope from writing and handing out those handbills of hers to the women around here. She's got my wife thinking, and too much thinking on Bessie's part comes to no good."

Mrs. Bradon sat up straighter on the wagon seat. "Women *do* think, Silas."

"Didn't say they didn't," Mr. Hanson answered. "But they ought to spend their thoughts on proper things, like raising children and cooking meals and making quilts—all good things for women to think about. I need my rest after a hard day's work. I don't need to hear Bessie going on and on about a woman's right to vote. What do women know about the way the world ought to be run?"

Suddenly a pretty young woman leaned out of an open upstairs window just over their heads. Strands of dark hair had escaped from the hairpins that held a twist on top of her head. She brushed them aside as she shouted, "Mr. Hanson, Elizabeth Cady Stanton is running for Congress in New York's eighth district. Running for Congress, mind you, and she can't even vote for herself! Is that fair? Is that honorable? Does it make any sense?"

Mr. Bradon smiled proudly at the young woman and called out, "Come on down, Penelope, and meet your new sister. Her name's Aggie."

Aggie gulped as Penelope's eyes met hers. Aggie was expecting to be judged, but Penelope only grinned.

"Aggie! Welcome! I'm so glad they chose a girl!" Her head popped out of sight, and in just a few minutes she burst through the front door. She helped her mother from the wagon, then Aggie, giving them both hugs.

She held Aggie's shoulders and looked into her eyes. "How do you feel about woman's suffrage, Aggie?"

"I . . . I don't know," Aggie said. "We didn't learn about that in the asylum. What is it?"

"Aha!" Penelope shouted. "I have a great deal to teach you!"

"Not now, dear," Mrs. Bradon said pleasantly. "Let's first of all show Aggie around the house and help her settle in. We'll give her the blue bedroom, next to yours."

Aggie picked up her bundle of clothing. She followed the women into the house while Mr. Bradon drove the wagon around toward the rear and Mr. Hanson rode off on his horse, sadly shaking his head.

The rooms of the house were warm and comfortable. The plump sofas and chairs were a little worn, but bright pillows were piled everywhere. A wide fireplace served as a wall between the parlor and kitchen, open to both rooms.

In the kitchen Sallie, the housekeeper, greeted Aggie. Sallie was tall and broad and blond. She had a wide, good-natured smile. As she stirred something in a huge iron pot, she said, "I hope you're good and hungry, Aggie. The bread's almost ready to come out of the oven, along with a pot roast and all the fixings."

Aggie's mouth watered. Meals here would be nothing like those served at the asylum. But before she let herself get carried away, she remembered her manners. She didn't want to be sent back to Mrs. Marchlander for being unhelpful to her new family.

"What can I do to help you?" she asked.

Sallie beamed. "Well, bless your little heart for asking." She fixed her gaze on Penelope. "The child's a good example for us all."

Aggie was warmed by a wave of relief. If she kept being helpful, she wouldn't be sent back to the asylum.

"I'll set the table," Penelope said quickly. "But first I need to show Aggie her bedroom." She clasped Aggie's hand and ran toward the stairs.

As they walked down the wide upstairs hallway, Aggie paused to glance at a carved wooden box that rested on a small table.

"That's Ma's doctoring box," Penelope said. "It's

full of clean cloth for bandages, ointment, liniment—things like that." She rolled her eyes to look upward. "Let's hope we never have to use it again."

"Again?" Aggie asked. "What—"

Without answering, Penelope threw open a door in the middle of the hallway. "Here's where you'll be sleeping," she said.

Aggie loved her bedroom. The iron bedstead was painted white, the walls were painted blue, and a quilt with bright squares of red, yellow, green, and blue lay across the bed. The drapes were opened wide so that sunlight shone through the large window, brightening the entire room.

Penelope bounced as she sat on the bed next to the bundle of Aggie's clothing. "This was my sister Grace's room," she said. "Grace went off to normal school. Now she teaches first grade in Chicago."

"Penelope and Leon and Grace," Aggie said. "How many of you are there?"

Penelope grinned again. "There's Albert, who went to California. He's an official with the railroad. Next comes Anne. She and her husband have five sons, and they went to west Kansas to homestead. Anne ran for mayor of the town they live in twice. She says when her boys are old enough to vote, she'll run again and win. My brothers Robert and Donald own a cattle ranch in Texas, and Arnold is thinking of running for governor in Iowa."

Aggie was impressed. With such outstanding children, Aggie hoped she wouldn't disappoint the Bradons.

Aggie untied her bundle of clothing. She hung the dress on a hook next to the bureau. The top bureau drawer was empty, so Aggie placed her change of underwear and nightgown inside. Then she slipped the note from her mother from her pocket and tucked it under the nightgown, where it would be safe. "With all those children, why did your parents want *me*?" Aggie asked.

"My parents like children," Penelope said. "Ma has been saying that she hates to see Leon grow up because none of her babies will be left."

Aggie wondered why she hadn't met Leon. "Where is Leon?" she asked. "Is he working on the farm?"

"Leon doesn't do farmwork," Penelope said.

"He's an inventor. He thinks up new machines or new ways of doing things that are better than the old ways."

Aggie had never met an inventor. It sounded exciting. "What is Leon inventing?" she asked.

Penelope smoothed down her skirt. "Well . . . Leon is the kind of inventor who is trying to help humanity. When he read that the supply of whale oil for lamps was getting low, he began working on a way to carry petroleum oil by pipeline to railroad depots, where it could be put directly into tank cars."

"That sounds like a good idea," Aggie said.

"It is. I mean, it was. It was so sensible somebody else thought of it first. Oil from the Pithole oil fields in Pennsylvania began being piped to the railroad a few months ago. So Leon had to think of something else to invent. Like his carpet broom."

"What kind of a broom is that?" Aggie asked.

"It's not exactly a broom. It's a row of brushes on a handle. You push them over a carpet. The brushes sweep crumbs from the carpet into a tray."

"I'd like to see that," Aggie said.

"You won't see Leon's," Penelope said. "Somebody else invented it first and just marketed it. It's called a carpet sweeper. So now Leon is working on something else."

She paused. "He's having a little trouble, though."

"What kind of trouble?"

"He's begun working on a chemical mixture that cloth can be soaked in. When the cloth dries, the chemicals will keep it from burning."

Aggie was impressed. "One of the matrons at the asylum got too close to the fire one evening, and the back of her skirt went up in flames. We ripped off her skirt, but she ran around shrieking in her drawers." Aggie giggled. "She wasn't hurt, but she was plenty mad about ruining a perfectly good dress. I'm glad Leon invented cloth that wouldn't burn."

"Oh, well, he didn't exactly," Penelope said. "Because of the accident."

"What accident?"

"You'll see when you meet him," Penelope said.

Aggie waited while Penelope ran her fingers through her hair, pulling out the long hairpins and sticking them back in again.

"What's Leon inventing now?" Aggie asked.

"An explosive," Penelope said quickly.

"You mean something that will blow up?"

"Sort of. In a way, that is." Penelope stood up and shook out her skirt. "Somebody named Alfred Nobel recently invented an explosive called dynamite. But dynamite is really powerful. It can blow up sides of mountains. Some of the farmers around here would like to blow up stumps of trees or large rocks imbedded in fields. But the idea of working with dynamite worries them. So Leon is experimenting in his laboratory to discover something that will do the job but not be as powerful as dynamite. Do you understand that?"

"I guess so," Aggie said. "But what's a laboratory?"

"It's where Leon keeps all his chemicals and tools—the place where he works." For just an instant Penelope looked worried. "Don't say anything about what I told you to Leon," she warned. "He has to keep his projects secret, so he can invent them before anyone else does. You and I are the only ones who know what he's doing."

"Your mother and father know, don't they?"

Penelope shrugged. "Not exactly," she said. "They've always encouraged all of us to follow our interests. They don't ask questions. They don't pry. And they never try to discourage us. So Leon doesn't see any need to tell them what he's working on."

"But what if he's wrong?" Aggie asked. "What if he invents something that's just as strong as dynamite? What if he makes a mistake and . . . ?"

Penelope chuckled. "Well, then he just starts all over again with something else!"

Chapter Eight

Suddenly an outside bell clanged.

Aggie jumped. "What's that?"

"The bell's used to call everyone," Penelope explained. "Right now the bell means it's time to eat!" She picked up her long skirts and raced out of the room and down the stairs. "I'm coming to set the table!" she yelled.

Aggie followed as quickly as she could.

Long tables had been placed together in a large room off the kitchen. As fast as she could, Penelope began setting the tables with plates, utensils, and napkins.

Sallie carried two large, steaming bowls of

potatoes into the room. She placed them with the sliced roast and vegetables that were already on the table.

As Aggie took a deep breath, her stomach rumbled. Nothing had ever smelled so delicious.

"Wash your hands," Sallie reminded Aggie.

When Aggie came to the table, Mr. Bradon welcomed her and made sure everyone had met her. Then he said a blessing over the food, and everyone began to eat.

Aggie was surprised that Sallie was seated at the end of the table, next to Mrs. Bradon. The hired hands were seated at the table too. Mrs. Marchlander would never have allowed any of the workers at the asylum to eat with her. But Mrs. Bradon chatted happily with Sallie as though they were good friends.

Aggie suddenly noticed that two places at the table were empty. She nudged Penelope, who was busy pouring gravy on her potatoes. Aggie's nudge was harder than she'd meant it to be. A glop of gravy landed on the tablecloth.

"Oh, no!" Aggie said. "I'm sorry!"

Sallie said, "The tablecloth will have to be washed anyway, gravy stains or no gravy stains."

"I don't mean to be so clumsy," Aggie added.

Penelope handed Aggie a large bowl of buttered beans. "You're not the only one," she said. "Better take this before I drop it."

Aggie filled her plate in silence. She felt terrible for having sloppy table manners.

A sudden loud clumping came from the stairway, and feet clattered across the floor. A tall, lanky boy flopped into the chair opposite Aggie. "Sorry I'm late," he said.

"Leon, this is your new sister, Aggie," Mrs. Bradon said.

Leon gave Aggie a quick look. "Hello," he said. "Glad to meet you." As fast as he could, he piled food on his plate and began to eat.

Aggie tried not to stare at Leon. He was the strangest-looking boy she'd ever seen. He had no eyelashes or eyebrows. He had plenty of dark, curly hair, but the hairline at his forehead was just a short, dark fuzz. It looked as if it had been burned off. *So that's what Penelope meant about the accident,* Aggie realized.

"How's your work going, Leon, dear?" Mrs. Bradon asked.

"Slowly," Leon said. "Very, very slowly." His mouth was filled with food; he gulped it down, then looked at his mother. "But I won't give up," he said. "I'm going to succeed."

"Good for you," Mrs. Bradon said. She beamed at him.

Mr. Bradon glanced at the other empty place. "Emmett," he said to one of the hired hands, "have you seen Uncle Louie?"

Emmett nodded. "Last time I saw him he was sawing firewood."

"Don't worry about Uncle Louie," Sallie said. "He'll come when he's good and ready." She lifted her head. "There's his whistle. He's on his way now."

Aggie lowered her fork and listened. She thought she heard a bird's trill. Then came the cry of one bird calling to another. A ruffle of low notes came to a sudden stop as the outer door opened, and a small, pear-shaped man with ruddy cheeks came into the room.

His eyes searched the faces at the table until they came to Aggie. "Ah," he said, and smiled broadly. "There's a new child in our family. Lovely, lovely."

"Aggie, this is Uncle Louie," Mr. Bradon said.

Aggie immediately jumped to her feet. She'd been told at the asylum that it was polite to stand when elders entered the room. "Hello, Mr. . . . uh . . . Mr. . . . ," she said.

"Just call me Uncle Louie," he told her. He held out the palm of his left hand to Aggie. On it rested a small wooden bird. "I made this for you," he said.

Aggie took the bird with wonder. Uncle Louie explained that he'd finish chopping the wood after the noon dinner. He'd come upon a piece of wood with a beautifully gnarled bend to it. He'd had to stop and find out what might be inside that piece of wood.

"After dinner," Penelope said, "I am going to teach Aggie about the woman suffrage movement."

"Not yet," Mrs. Bradon said. "After dinner I'd

like to read aloud to Aggie. Perhaps she'd like to read to me as well."

"I'm going to make sweet potato pie for supper," Sallie said to Aggie. "You can work alongside me and learn."

There were too many choices. Aggie didn't know which to take.

Uncle Louie shook his head. "All of you, let the girl get used to her new home," he said. "I'll show Aggie around the farm." He leaned forward, grinning. "There's a wonderful hill behind the duck pond. It's got a long, fine slope—perfect for rolling down."

Aggie gasped. "Rolling down a hill?"

"If you haven't tried it, it's about time you did," Uncle Louie said.

"Let's ask Aggie what she'd like to do," Mr. Bradon said.

Everyone looked at Aggie, who nervously twisted her fingers together. How could she answer? She didn't want to make the wrong choice. And she didn't want to offend anyone by choosing someone else.

Uncle Louie cocked his head, looking like the little fat-cheeked bird he had carved. He studied Aggie. "Aggie's coming with me," he said firmly. "Isn't that right, Aggie?"

"Yes," Aggie said. When no one protested, she let out a sigh of relief.

Aggie helped Sallie and Penelope take the plates from the table. They replaced them with bowls of cherry cobbler and pitchers of thick cream.

Aggie ate the delicious cobbler in silence. The Bradons seemed kind enough. As long as she behaved herself, they wouldn't send her away. And maybe she'd be able to make a place for herself in their home. . . . Maybe.

Chapter Nine

After lunch Aggie gently put her little wooden bird on a nearby table. Then she helped Penelope dry the stacks of dishes Sallie had washed. While Aggie worked, she listened to Uncle Louie imitating bird trills.

"How do you do that?" Aggie asked. "You make the same sound as a bird that used to perch in one of the trees outside the asylum in New Jersey."

"He must have been a mockingbird," Uncle Louie said. "Mockingbirds can make surprisingly beautiful sounds, especially when they're imitating other birds. Listen to the wood dove."

Low, soft notes floated through the kitchen.

Sallie dried her hands on a kitchen towel and

smiled at Uncle Louie. "I'd like to listen to you all day long, but someone's got to dump the soapsuds on the vegetable garden."

"Right away," Uncle Louie said. He hefted the heavy pan of water and carried it carefully out the door, which Sallie held open for him.

Sallie took the damp towel Aggie was holding. "Run along with him," she said. "He's ready to show you around the farm."

Aggie hesitated. She lowered her voice. "Uncle Louie said something about rolling down a hill. We aren't going to do that, are we?" There would be no way she could keep from getting grass stains on her dress. She didn't want to begin her stay at the Bradons by getting punished.

"You can roll down the hill only if you want to," Sallie answered.

"And you have every right to want to," Penelope said as she strode into the kitchen. "Why should boys get to roll down hills and not girls?"

"Ag-gie!" Uncle Louie called from outside the back door.

“Hold your horses! She’s coming,” Sallie hollered.

Aggie winced at all the noise. She hurried out the back door and down the steps to join Uncle Louie.

Uncle Louie led the way to the hayloft and taught Aggie how to pitch hay down to the empty horse stalls. He showed her how to find eggs where hens tried to hide them. And, out in the pasture, he bridled one of the older, gentler horses. Then he hoisted Aggie to the horse’s bare back and led Aggie and the horse through the low pasture.

Aggie delighted in the plodding movement of the horse and the way the breeze lifted the short tendrils of hair from her neck.

But soon Uncle Louie lifted Aggie down from the horse and led her up a nearby hill. He held his arms wide and declared, “Take a good look around. Isn’t this a beautiful world?”

Aggie sucked in her breath. Clouds dotted the bright blue sky like clumps of clotted cream. The Bradons’ house seemed far away, and the land between it and the hill was laid out like a patchwork quilt. Fields of growing things, some yellowed, some green, were edged by squares of rich brown earth. Stands of dark green pine and cedar created an uneven border. Below Aggie's feet, at the foot of the long, sloping hill, a small lake shimmered in the sunlight.

"Come on, Aggie," Uncle Louie shouted. "Let's roll down the hill!"

Without waiting for her, he flopped to the ground and hugged his arms to his chest. Away he rolled.

All Aggie could think about was what Mrs. Marchlander would say if she saw Aggie roll down the hill, her grass-stained skirt flying around her knees.

Aggie began walking primly down the hill, but her eyes were on Uncle Louie.

To Aggie's horror, Uncle Louie reached the bottom of the hill but kept rolling.

"Stop!" she cried, but Uncle Louie rolled right into the lake, landing in the shallow water with a splash.

"Are you hurt?" Aggie yelled. She ran down the hill toward him.

Aggie wasn't used to hills. Once she began running, she couldn't stop. She ran right into the lake, falling to her hands and knees in the shallow water. She gasped with surprise. She'd gotten her dress wet!

Uncle Louie sat up and smiled. "As long as we're here," he said, "why don't we try to catch frogs?"

His arm shot out of the water, and he held out a frog to Aggie. The frog bulged out its eyes, opened its mouth, and let out a deep croak. Uncle Louie imitated the frog. He looked and sounded just like it.

Aggie sat back in the water and began to laugh. She laughed until tears ran down her cheeks. Everything was so funny—the frog, Uncle Louie, and sitting in a lake.

Finally she wiped her eyes on the back of one sleeve. "I've never laughed like that before," she told Uncle Louie. "We weren't allowed to laugh or make noise at the asylum."

"Laughter is good for both mind and body," Uncle Louie said. "I'll make sure you have a good laugh every day."

Aggie grinned. "Just as long as it's not in the lake again," she said.

She looked down at her dress and was shocked at what she had done. Her happiness disappeared, and her throat felt dry and tight. "Mrs. Bradon won't like it that I've ruined my clothes," she said.

"The mud will wash out," Uncle Louie said. "Do you think you're the only one who's ended up in this duck pond?"

Imagining the entire Bradon family rolling down the hill and into the lake made Aggie laugh all over again.

Aggie grew quiet as she returned to the house. Surely she would be scolded for getting her clothes wet and muddy. She could picture how angry Mrs. Marchlander would be and what she would do.

But, to Aggie's surprise, no one in the Bradon household scolded her.

"Did you have a good time, dear?" Mrs. Bradon asked as she helped Aggie wash and change into the clothing she had brought with her.

"Yes, I did . . . but . . . ," Aggie began anxiously, "I'm sorry I got so muddy."

Mrs. Bradon just smiled. "There's no problem, dear. Sallie will scrub the mud from your clothes and lay them on bushes to dry in the sun."

"You aren't going to punish me?"

"Of course not. I'm glad that you and Uncle Louie had such fun."

Aggie was puzzled. Was Mrs. Bradon being sarcastic, the way Mrs. Marchlander had sometimes been? No, Aggie decided. Mrs. Bradon's smile seemed real. She seemed glad that Aggie had enjoyed herself.

"You have just this one change of clothing, so we'll find you some other things to wear," Mrs. Bradon said. "I'll go through some of the clothes the girls left behind. You can try them on."

There was a quick, light knock on the bedroom door. Before Mrs. Bradon could answer, Penelope opened the door.

"Alfie rode by, Ma," Penelope said. "He told me that the handbills are being printed. He'll see that they're delivered tonight."

"Very good," Mrs. Bradon said. "Then you'll have them for the rally next week."

Penelope nodded. "I'll take some of them into town first thing tomorrow morning," she said. "Aggie, will you come with me and help hand them out?"

"Yes," Aggie said quickly. She wanted to be helpful. But she had to ask, "What are handbills?"

Mrs. Bradon explained, "Handbills are sheets of paper on which information is printed."

"Very *important* information!" Penelope said. "These handbills have information about Elizabeth Cady Stanton's political campaign. And they tell women where they can write to ask for the right to vote." Penelope looked into Aggie's eyes. "You do want to help the cause, don't you?"

Aggie liked what Penelope was doing. She liked being asked to help her. And she liked the idea of someday being able to vote. If she could vote, her thoughts would matter. She'd have a say in how things were done. "Oh, yes! I want to help!" she answered.

Soon after breakfast the next morning, Aggie found herself in a small, two-wheeled carriage to which Penelope herself had hitched the horses.

"Why should I rely on a man to hitch up this trap?" Penelope told Aggie as they climbed into it. "A woman is every bit as capable as a man." She shoved a stack of handbills into Aggie's lap before she picked up the reins.

Aggie read the handbills as Penelope drove out of the Bradons' farm and onto the road to town. Just as Penelope had told her, the handbills urged women to support Elizabeth Cady Stanton's run for office by writing to their congressmen and asking for the right to vote.

"Missouri is a long way from New York," Aggie said. She thought about the tiring train journey she'd just had. "Will the women in Woodridge care if somebody named Elizabeth Cady Stanton wins an election in New York?"

"They *must* care!" Penelope cried. "In order for

the laws of this country to be fair, women must band together. If we do not, our cause is lost."

Penelope's voice rose excitedly as she said, "Our country's Declaration of Independence states that all *men* are created equal. Not *men and women.* It's hard to believe, but when it was written, Thomas Jefferson deliberately left out women."

The horse turned onto the main street of Woodridge, and a few passersby looked up and stared at Penelope. A few of them looked from Penelope to Aggie. A boy about seven or eight years old laughed and pointed at Aggie's hair. Then he stuck out his tongue. Bad memories from Aggie's trip west came flooding back, and she shrank back against the seat in embarrassment.

Penelope didn't seem to notice the onlookers or care that they were staring. "And look what happened when a group of *men* passed the Civil Rights amendment last April," she went on. "It was fair for Negro men to be given the vote. I have no quarrel with that. But what about Negro *women*? What about *all* women?"

Penelope pulled the buggy to a stop and jumped

out. As she tied the horse's lead to a hitching post, two women shoppers shifted the baskets on their arms and applauded.

But another woman scowled and pulled her skirts away, as if Penelope would get them dirty. "Penelope Bradon, you're behaving like a shameless hussy," she said. "What are you doing in town improperly dressed, without a hat?"

"I refuse to be a slave to fashions set by merchants who—for the most part—are men," Penelope answered. "I have no use for hats."

The woman's gaze shifted to Aggie, and she sniffed. "You should be ashamed of yourself, Penelope. You're setting a bad example for that poor, unfortunate orphan."

"She's not an orphan," Penelope said. "She's part of our family."

"I can't imagine what your parents were thinking of when they took in a child like that." The woman turned away, her heels clicking on the wooden sidewalk.

Aggie cringed as people turned to stare at her. That woman was as rude and unfair as Mrs. Marchlander. Aggie couldn't help it that she was an orphan, and she couldn't help how she looked.

She wanted to be like Penelope—not caring when people stared at her. It was hard for Aggie to speak, and when she did her voice cracked. But she jumped down from the trap and called after the woman. "Penelope has nothing to be ashamed of! She's only doing what she believes in."

Penelope grinned at Aggie. "And I believe in women's right to vote," she shouted to everyone in sight. "My sister Aggie will now assist me in giving all of you handbills that state our cause. We ask for your help and support. Come to our rally on Saturday morning!"

Some people took the handbills and stopped to ask Penelope questions. But many pushed the handbills away or threw them to the wooden sidewalk and stalked off. Aggie couldn't help hearing their rude comments.

"Women's right to vote? That's ridiculous. There isn't a woman alive who knows enough to vote."

"Penelope's a born old maid. She'll never get a husband."

"Unless he's as touched in the head as she is."

"If he is, he'd fit right in. All those Bradons are plumb crazy."

Aggie could feel her face growing hot and red with embarrassment and anger. "The Bradons aren't crazy! They aren't touched in the head! They're good, kind people!" she snapped.

As she whirled around to join Penelope, Aggie dropped the stack of handbills.

Someone began to laugh. Soon others joined in. Aggie tried to pick up the flyaway sheets of paper, clutching them to her chest.

Aggie was humiliated, not just for herself but for the Bradons. Couldn't the people in town see that the Bradons were fine people who just did things a little differently?

Chapter Ten

Aggie was silent on the ride home. But Penelope had so much to talk about, she didn't seem to notice.

When they arrived home, they found that Sallie had begun to make apple tarts. She called Aggie to join her, so Aggie washed her hands, stirred tablespoonfuls of water into the flour and shortening mixture with a fork, and rolled out the dough. She did everything exactly as she was told, but she let her mind escape to another place, just as she had done when she had work to do at the asylum.

She pictured Miss Kelly, smiling as she led a lovely young woman by the hand. Aggie could tell that the woman was smiling too, although her face was hidden in shadows. "Aggie," Miss Kelly said, "here is your mother. She is no longer in temporary distress, and she has come to find you."

"Oh!" Aggie realized she had spoken aloud when Sallie stopped chopping apples and looked at her.

"Are you all right?" Sallie asked. Her eyes were filled with concern.

"I—I was thinking about my mother," Aggie said. To her surprise, she found herself telling Sallie the story.

"My mother left me on the steps of a foundling home when I was ten days old. She left a note with my name and birth date. And she wrote that she loved me and didn't want to leave me, but she had to. She said she'd come back and get me, but she never did."

Tears rose in Sallie's eyes. "To leave her beautiful baby must have been the hardest thing your mother ever did."

Aggie looked up in surprise. "I've never been called beautiful. I've always been told I was plain. So I couldn't have been a beautiful baby."

"Of course you were beautiful," Sallie said. "All

babies are beautiful. And to your mother you were the most beautiful one of all. You can count on it."

"I wonder what my mother looked like. I wonder if she was beautiful too," Aggie said.

"If she had the same fair skin and dark hair that you do, then I'd say she was a mighty beautiful woman," Sallie answered.

"I think she must have been kind and quiet and gentle," Aggie said.

Sallie shook her head as she smiled at Aggie. "I'd agree with *kind*," she said, "but I think she was also a strong, courageous woman with spirit—like you."

"Like me?" In surprise Aggie spoke her thoughts aloud. Then she said the words that hurt so much to think about. "My mother said she would come back for me, but she never did."

Sallie sighed and put an arm around Aggie's shoulders. "Take my word for it, she would have come if she could."

"How could you know that?" Aggie cried out. She wished with all her heart that it were so. "How could anyone know?"

"Your mother took you to a place where she

knew you'd get good care, didn't she? And she left a note in her own words that she knew would comfort you, didn't she?" Sallie looked deeply into Aggie's eyes as she added, "Your mother was a good mother who loved her baby. Believe me. She would have come if she could."

Over and over the words trickled through Aggie's mind like the soft notes of a comforting song: *She would have come if she could.* Now she had a new secret to carry within her heart.

Handing Aggie the jar of sugar and a spoon, Sallie said, "Let's get back to work so those tarts'll be done by suppertime."

She showed Aggie how to mix sugar and cinnamon and stir the mixture into the apples, filling each tart shell and dotting the apples with butter.

Aggie put on the top crusts, carefully pinching the edges together, but her mind was with her mother—her beautiful mother. Were she and her mother really alike, as Sallie had said? Her mother would have loved her no matter how she behaved. Would the Bradons? Aggie shivered. She was afraid to find out.

Aggie helped Sallie carry the pans of tarts outside to the brick oven in the summer kitchen. As Sallie straightened, one hand pressing against the small of her back, she asked, "Did you have a good time in town with Penelope?"

Aggie had liked what Penelope said and did, but she hadn't liked the rude stares and comments from the people in town. "Some people liked what Penelope talked about, but a lot of people didn't," she said.

"That's not surprising. Bring up anything, and you'll find some people dead set against it."

Aggie went on. "A woman scolded Penelope because she wasn't wearing a hat."

Sallie chuckled. "Once Mrs. Hanson told Penelope that if she didn't wear a hat her skin would get browned and freckled, and she'd never catch herself a husband. Ever since that time Penelope wouldn't be caught dead wearing a hat."

Aggie realized that she must have looked surprised, because Sallie said, "Didn't you ever *not* do something just because some busybody insisted that you do it?"

"I guess so," Aggie said. "I was always getting into trouble at the asylum because I did things the way I thought they *should* be done. Only, by doing things that way, I got punished for breaking the rules."

"I figured you had a mind of your own," Sallie said. "There's a good reason you got matched up with the Bradons. You'll fit right in here."

Aggie wanted to believe Sallie. She smiled shakily. "I hope I can."

When the tarts were in the oven, Aggie washed her hands and left the kitchen. The downstairs was completely quiet. Mrs. Bradon was sound asleep in her rocking chair, an open book upside down on her lap. There was no sign of Mr. Bradon and Uncle Louie. Aggie guessed they were outside doing farmwork.

Aggie climbed the stairs and saw that Penelope's door was wide open. But Penelope was nowhere in sight. Maybe she was with Leon. Aggie knew that Leon would be in his laboratory in the attic.

She silently went to her room. She sat on the bed wishing she could do some of the interesting things the Bradons did. She'd love to be as brave as Penelope and help give speeches for women's right to vote. She'd love to invent things. She'd love to learn how to whistle like a bird. Aggie smiled as she thought that she'd even love to forget getting dirty and roll down the hill. But how could she do these things and still be the well-behaved daughter the Bradons wanted?

Mrs. Bradon called from the stairs, "Aggie, dear? Are you busy?"

Aggie leaped to her feet and ran into the hallway. "No, Mrs. Bradon. What would you like me to do?" she asked.

"I thought it would be nice to invite some friends in on Sunday afternoon and entertain them with a few tableaux."

Aggie was puzzled. "What are tableaux?"

Mrs. Bradon's eyes sparkled. "Let me see, how can I best explain?" she said. "A tableau is a scene. The people in the scene are dressed in costumes. They don't move or talk. They simply present a living picture."

"A picture of what?" Aggie asked.

"Of whatever is being read. Usually it's a short poem." Mrs. Bradon smiled modestly. "I do so love to read poetry," she said. "Presenting tableaux to our friends and serving cake and tea afterward—that's one of our family traditions."

"I'll be glad to help you serve," Aggie said.

"Oh, no, dear," Mrs. Bradon said. "You can be one of the figures in a tableau. I thought perhaps that I could read John Keats's 'Ode on a Grecian Urn,' and you could stand posed as a figure on that urn. If you wear a garland of leaves on your head and I drape a white tablecloth about your shoulders—"

In horror Aggie clapped her hands to her face. If she were dressed in a tablecloth, people would laugh. "In front of your family? Your friends?"

Mrs. Bradon said, "You'll love the tableaux, Aggie. They're great fun. Uncle Louie is eager to do Longfellow's 'The Wreck of the Hesperus.' He suggested that you might take the part of the skipper's little daughter." She smiled at Aggie with delight. "Just remember, dear, this is your family, and our friends will soon be yours, too."

"But I've never done this before," Aggie cried. "What if I make a mistake? What if I ruin the tableaux?"

Mrs. Bradon chuckled. "You can't ruin them, Aggie dear. Believe me, you'll have great fun. We all laugh and have a marvelous time."

Aggie's knees wobbled, and she sank into the nearest chair. She couldn't stand up in front of a group of people while they stared and laughed at her. She couldn't!

Chapter Eleven

Penelope had woven strands of a jasmine vine into a wreath.

Mrs. Bradon placed it on Aggie's head. Then she pinned and adjusted a tablecloth, tying it at Aggie's waist. She stood back and admired Aggie. "Absolutely perfect!" she said.

"Maybe she could hold an urn on her head," Penelope said.

"No," Mrs. Bradon said. "We don't have anything that looks like an urn. I think she should be staring into the distance."

"How about the glass pitcher?" Penelope asked.

For the first time Aggie dared to speak up. "Why

don't you take my place?" she asked Penelope. "You'd be a lot better at this than I would."

"I don't hold still long enough," Penelope answered.

"That's all right, Penelope dear," Mrs. Bradon said. "You'll be included. I've found a short poem for your tableau—Robert Browning's 'My Last Duchess.' You can look very regal. Just pretend you're giving one of your speeches."

Aggie began to feel a little better. "Will Penelope have to wear a tablecloth too?" she asked.

"No. In a box somewhere we have some old red velvet drapes with gold fringe. I'm sure we can do something regal with those," Mrs. Bradon answered.

Aggie nodded. Penelope wrapped in dusty old drapes might look even worse than Aggie would dressed in a tablecloth. "What is Leon going to wear?" she asked.

"Leon doesn't attend tableaux anymore," Penelope said. She made a face. "He says he's too busy being an inventor." She broke into laughter. "The last time Leon was in a tableau, he was a sea captain.

He climbed up to the bridge of his ship with his telescope. But the bridge was a chair with a caned seat, and Leon's foot went right through. He hopped around with one leg stuck in the chair, yelling at everyone."

"You might say he *sounded* like a sea captain," Mrs. Bradon said. She laughed too.

Aggie couldn't help smiling at the idea of Leon hopping around with his leg stuck in a chair, but she didn't laugh. She didn't blame Leon for not wanting to be in a tableau, with everyone staring and laughing. She didn't want to be either. The idea made her stomach hurt.

During the rehearsal everyone grew silly—everyone except Aggie, who did everything Mrs. Bradon told her to do. Penelope kept changing her pose as an elegant duchess, and each pose was more ridiculous than the one before. Uncle Louie made such funny faces that Sallie laughed until she got the hiccups.

"Behave yourselves," Mrs. Bradon kept saying, although she couldn't keep from laughing either.

After church services on Sunday, a number of people came to greet the Bradons. Among them was a tall, broad-shouldered man who smiled down at Aggie.

"I'm Andrew MacNair," he said. "The Bradons sent for me. They invited me to come to their tableaux this afternoon. I understand you're going to take part."

Aggie's knees shook, and for a moment she could hardly see Mr. MacNair's face. The Bradons had sent for him! Aggie gulped down a knot of fear that threatened to choke her. Did this mean that the Bradons didn't want her? Had Andrew MacNair come to take her away?

Cold with fear, Aggie somehow managed to get through dinner. She busied herself by setting up chairs for the afternoon's guests. But she was unable to smile as she helped to greet the guests. Their names were blurs in her mind, except for one. The rude boy she had seen in town was there with his parents, Mr. and Mrs. Hanson. When he thought no one but Aggie was aware, he made a face at her.

But Uncle Louie had seen him. He bent down,

made an even more horrible face, and said, "Hello there, Silas Junior. You're looking your usual self."

Silas Junior tried to kick Aggie's shins, but at that moment Uncle Louie turned him around and plopped him down into a chair. "Enjoy the program," Uncle Louie said.

"Hello, Aggie," Mr. MacNair said.

Aggie mumbled a greeting, but she couldn't meet his eyes. She didn't want him to take her from the Bradons. Maybe they'd change their minds. Maybe they'd keep her, if only she did her best during the tableaux.

"Ode on a Grecian Urn" was first on the program. Aggie stood stiffly, trying not to look at the audience—especially at Silas Junior, who kept snickering. She knew she looked strange, draped in the white tablecloth, with the wreath of leaves tickling her forehead. But she had to be good. She had to do her job well. Aggie was glad when the poem ended.

Uncle Louie and Sallie went next. Sallie wore what was supposed to be a ballgown, and as she took her place she kept tripping on the long skirt.

Uncle Louie wore a sword fastened to his belt and a broad red sash across his chest. The two of them posed as though they were dancing, while Mrs. Bradon read the poem "Lochinvar."

" 'O, young Lochinvar is come out of the West,' " Mrs. Bradon began. The audience giggled.

Soon their giggles became roars of laughter as Uncle Louie winked at the blushing Sallie and Mrs. Bradon read, " 'So faithful in love, and so dauntless in war/There never was knight like the young Lochinvar.' "

How dare they laugh at Uncle Louie? Aggie thought. But Uncle Louie seemed to be enjoying the laughter. Even Sallie was laughing.

Then, to her surprise, Aggie realized that the audience wasn't laughing *at* Uncle Louie. They were laughing *with* him. Aggie wished she could laugh too. But she had a sick feeling in her stomach. How could she join in the fun when this might be her last day with the Bradons?

As the poem ended, the audience clapped and cheered. Uncle Louie and Sallie bowed and left the corner of the room that served as stage. Penelope, wearing the dark red velvet drapes pinned together and all her mother's jewelry, climbed onto a box and struck a dramatic pose.

" 'That's my last Duchess painted on the wall,/ Looking as if she were alive,' " Mrs. Bradon read.

Silas Junior hooted and shouted, "Looking like she was going to give another speech, you mean!"

His parents laughed.

Aggie flushed with anger, but Mrs. Bradon just kept reading. " 'She had/A heart—how shall I say?—too soon made glad,/Too easily impressed; she liked whate'er/She looked on. . . .' "

"Not Penelope," Silas Junior said. "Penelope only likes to give speeches."

Aggie couldn't take any more of Silas Junior's rudeness. She didn't care anymore about being quiet and obedient. She jumped to her feet and stood in front of Penelope, protecting her. "Don't talk like that about Penelope!" Aggie cried. She tried to remember the things Penelope had said. "Penelope is speaking for women! She's fighting for their rights!"

Aggie threw out her arms dramatically as she

spoke, just the way Penelope had. Unfortunately, she was too close to Penelope, and she accidentally hit her in the stomach.

"Ooof!" Penelope grunted. She doubled over and fell off the box and onto Aggie. They tumbled into a heap on the floor.

Aggie sat up and looked at Penelope, who was struggling to sit up while pulling a strand of gold fringe from her mouth. Penelope began to laugh. She whooped with laughter.

It *was* funny. Aggie couldn't resist. She threw back her head and joined in the laughter.

Soon everybody in the audience was laughing. And Aggie knew they were laughing *with* her. She was a part of it all. She was part of the Bradons.

Mrs. Bradon sat on the floor and hugged Aggie. "Oh, Aggie, we knew the moment we saw you that you would be a very special daughter," she said.

Aggie looked at the smiling people who were gathered around her. The Bradons might be different from their neighbors, maybe even a little strange—but so was she.

"Do you mean you aren't going to send me back?" Aggie asked Mrs. Bradon.

"Send you back? Never!" Mrs. Bradon hugged her again.

"We'd like to officially adopt you, Aggie," Mr. Bradon said. "That's why we asked Andrew MacNair to come today. Since he approves, all we need to do is go to the county seat and sign the papers to give you our name."

"Please think about it, Aggie," Mrs. Bradon said. "If this is what you would like, just tell us when you're ready."

"I don't have to think about it," Aggie answered. "I'm ready right now."

Agatha Mae Bradon. Aggie grinned. She knew that her mother would have liked that name.

EPILOGUE

AGGIE'S LETTER TO FRANCES MARY KELLY

Dear Miss Kelly,

Do you remember the note I told you about? The note my mother left with me at the foundling home? My mother asked that I be given loving care until she came for me.

I don't know why my mother didn't come. Sallie said she would have if she could, and I feel better thinking about that. I don't know where my mother is, or even if she is still living. But I'm sure she'd love the Bradons as much as I do.

The Bradons aren't like everybody else. Sometimes people stare at them and make rude comments because they're different. It's the same thing some people do to me. The Bradons don't care. They're happy being themselves. I'm not going to care, either. I like being myself, and I like being one of the Bradons. As soon as we can go to the courthouse and sign the papers, the Bradons are going to adopt me.

Thank you for bringing me to Missouri to find my family.

Devotedly,

Agatha Mae Bradon

Glossary

bureau ***byoor′ o*** A chest of drawers.

carpetbag ***kar′ pit bag*** A bag for traveling, made of carpet.

confidential ***kon fi den′ shul*** Kept secret.

distress ***di stres′*** A state of trouble, anxiety, or sorrow.

drawers ***drors*** Underpants with legs.

foundling home ***found′ ling home*** A place set up to care for abandoned or orphaned children.

gruel ***grool*** A thin cereal of oatmeal boiled in water or milk.

handbill ***hand′ bil*** A printed announcement, given out by hand.

housekeeper ***hous′ ke per*** A woman who is hired to do or direct the work in a home.

matron ***ma' tron*** A woman serving as an attendant in an institution.

normal school ***nor' mal school*** A school offering a two-year teacher training course to high-school graduates. The first opened in 1823.

orphan asylum ***or' fan a si' lum*** An institution to care for children without parents.

rally ***ral' e*** Drawing people together for a common cause.

routine ***roo ten'*** Doing something the same way over and over.

soot ***soot*** Airborne tiny black particles from burning coal or wood.

strapping ***strap' ing*** Large and strong, as in describing a person.

tableau, tableaux ***tab lo', tab loz'*** People dressed in costumes, posed to make a scene from a story, poem, or painting.

temporary ***tem′ po rer e*** For a time only, not lasting.

waif ***waf*** A child who has no home.

woman suffrage ***woom′ en suf′ rij*** The movement to give women the right to vote in elections.

The Story of the Orphan Trains

In 1850 there were five hundred thousand people living in New York City. Ten thousand of these people were homeless children.

Many of these children were immigrants—they had come to the United States with their families from other countries. Many lived in one-room apartments. These rooms had stoves for heating and cooking, but the only water was in troughs in the hallways. These apartments were called tenements, and they were often crowded together in neighborhoods.

Immigrant parents worked long hours for very low wages. Sometimes they had barely enough money to buy food. Everyone in the family over the age of ten was expected to work. Few of these children could attend school, and many could not read or write.

Girls took in bundles of cloth from clothing

New York City's Lower East Side during the late nineteenth century.
Courtesy the Children's Aid Society

manufacturers. They carefully sewed men's shirts, women's blouses, and babies' gowns. Or they made paper flowers and tried to sell them on the busy streets.

Boys shined shoes or sold newspapers.

There were no wonder medicines in the 1800s. Many immigrants who lived in poor conditions died from contagious diseases. Children often became orphans with no one to care for them.

Some orphaned children were taken in by aunts and uncles. But many of the immigrant children had no relatives to come to their aid. They had left their grandparents, aunts, and uncles in other countries. They were alone. No one in the government had developed any plans for caring for them.

These orphans were evicted from their homes so that the rooms could be rented to other families. Orphans with no homes and no beds slept in alleys.

This was a time in which children were expected to work hard, along with adults. They were expected to take care of themselves. But there were not enough jobs for all the orphans in New York

A New York City "street arab."
Courtesy the Children's Aid Society

City. Many street arabs, as they were called, turned to lives of crime.

Charles Loring Brace, a young minister and social worker, became aware of this situation. He worried about these children, who so badly needed care. With the help of some friends, he founded the Children's Aid Society. The Children's Aid Society provided a place to live for some of the homeless children. It also set up industrial schools to train the children of the very poor in job skills.

Charles Loring Brace soon realized, however, that these steps were not enough. He came up with the idea of giving homeless, orphaned children a second—and much better—chance at life by taking them out of the city and placing them in homes in rural areas of the country.

Brace hired a scout to visit some of the farm communities west of New York State. He asked the scout to find out if people would be interested in taking orphan children into their homes. The scout was surprised by how many people wanted the children.

One woman wrote, "Last year was a very hard

Charles Loring Brace, founder of the Children's Aid Society and the orphan train program.
Courtesy the Children's Aid Society

A boy proudly holds up his Children's Aid Society membership card.
Courtesy the Children's Aid Society

year, and we lost many of our children. Yes, we want your children. Please send your children."

Brace went to orphans who were living on the streets and told them what he wanted to do. Children flocked to the Children's Aid Society office. "Take me," they begged. "Please take me."

"Where do you live?" the children were asked.

The answer was always the same: "Don't live no-where."

The first orphan train was sent west in 1856, and the last one in 1929. During these years more than a hundred and fifty thousand children were taken out of New York City by the Children's Aid Society. Another hundred thousand children were sent by train to new homes in the West by the New York Foundling Home. By 1929 states had established welfare laws and had begun taking care of people in need, so the orphan trains were discontinued.

Before a group of children was sent west by train, notices that the children were coming would be placed in the newspapers of towns along the route: "WANTED: HOMES FOR CHILDREN," one notice said. It then listed the Society's rules. Children were to be treated as members of the family. They were to be taken to church on Sundays and sent to school until they were fourteen.

Handbills were posted in the towns where the orphan train stopped, where people could easily see them. One said: "CHILDREN WITHOUT HOMES. A

Boys on board an orphan train.
Courtesy the Children's Aid Society

number of the Children brought from New York are still without homes. Friends from the country, please call and see them."

A committee of local citizens would be chosen at each of the towns. The members of the committee were given the responsibility of making sure that the

TERMS ON WHICH BOYS ARE PLACED IN HOMES.

ALL APPLICANTS MUST BE ENDORSED BY THE COMMITTEE

Boys fifteen years old are expected to work till they are eighteen for their board and clothes. At the end of that time they are at liberty to make their own arrangements.

Boys between twelve and fifteen are expected to work for their board and clothes till they are eighteen, but must be sent to school a part of each year, after that it is expected that they receive wages.

Boys under twelve are expected to remain till they are eighteen, and must be treated by the applicants as one of their own children in matters of schooling, clothing and training.

Should a removal be necessary it can be arranged through the committee or by writing to the Agent.

The Society reserves the right of removing a boy at any time for just cause.

We desire to hear from every child twice a year.

All Expenses of Transportation are Paid by the Society.

CHILDREN'S AID SOCIETY.
24 ST. MARKS PLACE, N.Y.

E. TROTT, AGENT.

Families that wanted to adopt an orphan train rider had to follow rules such as these.

Courtesy the Children's Aid Society

people who took the orphan train children in were good people.

Most committee members tried to do a good job. But sometimes a child was placed in a home that turned out to be unhappy. Some farmers wanted free labor and were unkind to the boys they chose. But there were many good people who wanted to provide loving homes for the orphans. Many people were so happy with their children that they took a step beyond being foster parents and legally adopted them.

Not all the children who were taken west on the orphan trains were orphans. Some had one or both parents still living. But sometimes fathers and mothers brought their children to the Children's Aid Society.

"I can't take care of my children," they would say. "I want them to have a much better life than I can give them. Please take them west to a new home."

What did the orphan train children think about their new lives? What made the biggest impression on them? They were used to living in small spaces, surrounded by many people in a noisy, crowded city. Were they overwhelmed by the sight of miles of open countryside?

Many of them had never tasted an apple. How did they react when they saw red apples growing on trees?

When they sat down to a meal with their new families, did they stuff themselves? And did they

A group of children ready to board the orphan trains, and their placing-out agents.
Courtesy the Children's Aid Society

feel a little guilty, remembering the small portions of food their parents had to eat?

Were they afraid to approach the large farm animals? What was it like for them to milk a cow for the first time?

WHAT IS NEEDED

Money is needed to carry forward this great child-saving enterprise. With more confidence do we ask it, since it has been so clearly shown that this work of philanthropy is not a dead weight upon the community. Though its chief aim is to rescue the helpless child victims of our social errors, it also makes a distinct economic return in the reduction of the number of those who are hopeless charges upon the common purse. More money at our command means more power to extend this great opportunity of help to the many homeless children in the boys' and girls' lodging houses in New York, and in the asylums and institutions throughout the State. We therefore ask the public for a more liberal support of this noble charity, confident that every dollar invested will bring a double return in the best kind of help to the children, so pitifully in need of it.

TABLE SHOWING THE NUMBER OF CHILDREN AND POOR FAMILIES SENT TO EACH STATE

State	Number	State	Number
New York	33,053	North Dakota	975
New Jersey	4,977	South Dakota	43
Pennsylvania	2,679	Kentucky	212
Maryland	563	Georgia	317
Delaware	833	Tennessee	233
District of Columbia	172	Mississippi	210
Canada	566	Florida	600
Maine	43	Alabama	50
New Hampshire	136	North Carolina	144
Vermont	262	South Carolina	191
Rhode Island	340	Louisiana	70
Massachusetts	375	Indian Territory	59
Connecticut	1,588	Oklahoma	95
Ohio	7,272	Arkansas	136
Indiana	3,955	Montana	83
Illinois	9,172	Wyoming	19
Iowa	6,675	Colorado	1,563
Missouri	6,088	Utah	31
Nebraska	3,442	Idaho	52
Minnesota	3,258	Washington	231
Kansas	4,150	Nevada	59
Michigan	5,326	Oregon	90
Wisconsin	2,750	California	168
Virginia	1,634	New Mexico	1
West Virginia	149	Texas	1,527

This chart, from the Children's Aid Society's 1910 bulletin, shows the number of children who rode the orphan trains and the states to which they were sent.

Courtesy the Children's Aid Society

Three sisters who were taken in by the Children's Aid Society after their mother had died. At the time the photograph was taken, the two youngest girls had been adopted.
Courtesy the Children's Aid Society

During the first few years of the orphan trains, the records kept by the Children's Aid Society were not complete. In a later survey taken in 1917, the Children's Aid Society researched what had happened to many of the orphan train children who had grown up.

He found that among them were a governor of North Dakota, a governor of the Territory of Alaska, two members of the United States Congress, nine members of state legislatures, two district attorneys, two mayors, a justice of the Supreme Court, four judges, many college professors, teachers, journalists, bankers, doctors, attorneys, four army officers, and seven thousand soldiers and sailors.

Although there were some problems in this system of matching homeless children with foster parents, the orphan train program did what it set out to do. It gave the homeless children of New York City the chance to live much better lives.

Woman Suffrage Movement

In this book Penelope Bradon tells Aggie about "woman suffrage," or the right of women to vote. Women in the United States did not universally have the right to vote until 1920, when the Nineteenth Amendment to the Constitution was passed. Before then women had been given the right to vote in Wyoming and Utah. And in nineteen states women were given partial voting rights—for example, the right to vote only in local elections.

The women's suffrage movement was part of a larger campaign for women's rights in America. Women wanted equal rights with men in a variety of areas—marriage, education, religion, politics, and jobs. Many of the women who joined together to fight for women's rights also had in common abolitionist, or antislavery, beliefs.

Three of the most famous women in the battle for women's rights and suffrage were Lucretia Mott, Elizabeth Cady Stanton, and Susan B. Anthony. Lucretia Mott was born in Nantucket, Massachu-

A woman and her daughter in their New York City tenement.
Courtesy the Children's Aid Society

setts, in 1790. She was a teacher, a lecturer, and a minister, as well as the founder of the Philadelphia Female Anti-Slavery Society. Elizabeth Cady Stanton was born in Johnstown, New York, in 1815. She was an abolitionist who helped begin the woman suffrage movement when she and Lucretia Mott organized the first women's rights meeting in 1848, in Seneca Falls, New York. Susan B. Anthony was born in Adams, Massachusetts, in 1820. She was active in the temperance (moderation in or abstinence from alcohol), abolitionist, and woman suffrage movements.

The meeting in Seneca Falls was one of the most important events in the history of woman suffrage. At this meeting a "Declaration of Sentiments" was drawn up and signed. The document demanded equal rights for women, including the right to vote.

After the Civil War Elizabeth Cady Stanton joined Susan B. Anthony and in 1869 formed the National Woman Suffrage Association (NWSA). The NWSA accepted only women as members, and along with fighting for women's suffrage, they opposed the Fifteenth Amendment to the Constitution, which gave only black men—and not black women—the right to vote. A rival group, the American Woman Suffrage Association, formed at the same time. In 1890 these two groups united to form the National American Woman Suffrage Association (NAWSA), which was able to finally win the right to vote for women. In 1920, the same year that American women were given the right to vote, the NAWSA became the League of Women Voters. The League is still in existence, and its mission is to encourage all American citizens to participate actively in their government by informed voting.

SOURCES:

The Reader's Companion to American History, Eric Foner and John A. Garraty, Ed. Boston, 1991: Houghton Mifflin Company.

Webster's New Biographical Dictionary, Springfield, Mass., 1988: Merriam-Webster Inc.

The Children's Aid Society is still active today, helping more than 100,000 New York City children and their families each year. The Society's services include adoption and foster care, medical and dental care, counseling, preventive services, winter and summer camps, recreation, cultural enrichment, education, and job training.

For more information, contact:

The Children's Aid Society
105 East 22nd Street
New York, NY 10010

About the Author

Joan Lowery Nixon is the acclaimed author of more than a hundred books for young readers. She has served as president of the Mystery Writers of America and as regional vice-president for the Southwest Chapter of that society. She is the only four-time winner of the Edgar Allan Poe Best Juvenile Mystery Award given by the Mystery Writers of America. She is also a two-time winner of the Golden Spur Award, which she won for *A Family Apart* and *In the Face of Danger,* the first and third books of the Orphan Train Adventures, which also include *Caught in the Act, A Place to Belong, A Dangerous Promise, Keeping Secrets,* and *Circle of Love.* She was moved by the true experiences of the children on the nineteenth-century orphan trains to research and write the Orphan Train Adventures, as well as the Orphan Train Children books, which also include *Lucy's Wish, Will's Choice* and *David's Search.*

Joan Lowery Nixon and her husband live in Houston.